SCHOOL CRUSH

HITEN BAREJA

To my little kitten, my best friend, thank you for
your endless support and motivation.

Copyright page

This book has been self-published with all reasonable efforts taken to make the material error-free by the author. No part of this book shall be used, reproduced in any manner whatsoever without written permission from the author, except in the case of brief quotations embodied in critical articles and reviews.

The Author of this book is solely responsible and liable for its content including but not limited to the views, representations, descriptions, statements, information, opinions and references ["Content"]. The Content of this book shall not constitute or be construed or deemed to reflect the opinion or expression of the Publisher or Editor. Neither the Publisher nor Editor endorse or approve the Content of this book or guarantee the reliability, accuracy or completeness of the Content published herein and do not make any representations or warranties of any kind, express or implied, including but not limited to the implied warranties of merchantability, fitness for a particular purpose. The Publisher and Editor shall not be liable whatsoever for any errors, omissions, whether such errors or omissions result from negligence, accident, or any other cause or claims for loss or damages of any kind, including without limitation, indirect or consequential loss or damage arising out of use, inability to use, or about the reliability, accuracy or sufficiency of the information contained in this book.

Preface

We all have or had a crush on someone or something in our school life. Boys have a crush on girls, girls too have a crush on boys, toppers have a crush on their grades etc.

'School Crush' covers the story of a boy, Ahaan, who falls in love with Aanya, his junior. He developed a crush on her but what about the challenges he was going to face because love demands time and efforts. He's in 12th standard and had board exams this year. Will he be able to manage his love along with his studies? Well, some incidents, written in the book are based on my school life but I can say, you'll like them while reading.

Read the book and once again, get lost in your school days when you too had a crush on someone.

With love,

Hiten Bareja

Acknowledgements

I extend my heartfelt gratitude to my Mom and Dad for their unconditional love and support. Special thanks to my sister for her encouragement. To my readers, your enthusiasm boosts up my passion for writing. Last but not the least, a big thanks to my best friend who always supported me in everything and kept me motivated throughout this journey.

1
School assembly

Bell rings. Drum beats started. Today, there was a special assembly for Independence day in our school. All the children were leaving their class rooms and heading towards the assembly ground in a proper line. Our class teacher, Mrs. Ankita Shukla, ordered us to make a line and move towards the assembly ground.

We reached the assembly ground and made two separate lines, one for boys and other for girls in increasing order of height. I was not much taller than my friends, so I was standing at the third position from the front. Children from other classes were also standing there.

"Standeeteeze", our sports teacher, Mr. Anant Dudeja shouted. Yes, he speaks very bad English and that's why he doesn't even know that it's 'stand at ease' not 'standeeteeze'.

We all followed his instructions.

I looked back and saw my friends giggling and having fun. I wish my height was a little longer. Suddenly I heard a very sweet voice coming from the speakers.

"Good morning! Our respected principal ma'am, Vice principal sir, teachers and all the students present here. Today....."

Someone interrupted. "Ahaan.", said Dhiraj softly. Dhiraj was my best friend since 10th standard. We had a lot of fun together and now he was no less than a brother to me.

"Come back.", he said.

"Wait.", I replied.

I turned back to see the owner of that sweet voice and I saw a girl, conducting the assembly. She was looking damn beautiful. I was standing nearly 20 feet away from that girl but still I could say that she had very pretty and innocent eyes. I was a boy who didn't want to get into a relationship at that time because of my last heartbreak, but it was very difficult to stop myself from falling in love again after seeing her.

"Ahaan, are you coming or not?", said Dhiraj again.

I went back but my entire focus was on that girl. This might be the first time that I listened to the entire assembly attentively.

2
Instagram

Two months later. Since that day, I had never seen that girl again in school. I had not forgotten her but there was no reason to miss her.

One day, I was using Instagram just like every other day. I was scrolling through the reels and laughing. Suddenly I got a message from my friends group. 'The Stepdads'. Yes that was the name of our group. Just one of 'The Boys' things.

Karan : Let's go out somewhere.

Ahaan : I'm ready.

Dhiraj : But where?

Farhan : I'm going to sleep, you guys go.

Farhan was that boy in our group who only liked sleeping. He can literally sleep anytime, anywhere.

Karan : Shut up! *Kumbhkaran*.

Ahaan : Chilli potato?

Dhiraj : Done.

Karan : Be there by 7 PM and don't get late.

It was 6.40 PM. They had told me to come but I knew that one of them would definitely be late. So I started using Instagram again. I was watching people's stories. After 2 stories, I saw a photograph.

In that photograph, there were 5 girls. One of them was my follower and my junior, Ritu. Of the remaining 4 girls, one was the same girl whom I had seen in the assembly that day.

I instantly recognised her. There were four IDs mentioned over there. I started looking at those IDs one by one.

The first one was, 'Manvi_23'. I opened her ID and looked at her profile. She was not that girl. Similarly I did with the other three IDs. I doubted two IDs because there was no profile picture in both of them. One of them was 'Sanya__09' and the other one was 'Aanya.04'.

I was confused as to which of these two girls could be that girl. Just as I was thinking, I got a call. It was Dhiraj. I picked it up.

Dhiraj : Where are you? We have reached.

Ahaan : I'm just arriving, I'm on my way.

Dhiraj : Be quick, asshole.

3
Third Party

It was 8.38 PM. I just came home after hanging out with my friends.

"Just keep loitering. Don't study.", said my mom, Mrs. Kriti Sehgal.

"Okay mom. I'll study...", I said. "But it would have been okay if I had something to eat before studying.", I grinned.

"Shameless.", my mother taunted me.

"Hehe"

I went inside my room and changed my clothes. After 20 minutes, my mother gave me my dinner. I usually have dinner in my room only. When I was having dinner, I remembered those two IDs and once again, I became confused and started overthinking.

I thought about that girl and that day, all night. I even thought what could be the name of that girl, based on her appearance. Thinking about this, I felt sleepy and went to sleep.

ᗛᗛᗛ

The next day, I woke up, attended my school and came back home. The whole time I was thinking about how to find out what her ID was. Suddenly, I came up with an idea. What if I met her through a common friend? But the problem was that, I didn't know who our common friend was. I kept thinking, and thinking, and thinking.

After thinking for nearly 20 minutes, I remembered a girl. Her name was Divya Gupta and she was one of the most famous girls of our school because of her achievements and a good friend of mine too.

I thought of taking her help but I still had a lot of questions in my mind, like, 'Should I tell her, that I had a crush on her?', 'Will she judge me?', 'Does she know that girl or am I wasting my time?' etc. I started overthinking again. Nevertheless, I messaged her.

Ahaan : Hi.

After waiting for about 10 minutes.

Divya : Hey.

Ahaan : Actually I need your help.

Divya : Is everything okay?

Ahaan : Yeah. Actually...

Divya : Actually?

Ahaan : You'll judge me for sure.

Divya : Why would I judge you? Tell me.

Ahaan : Okay. So, do you know that girl, who conducted the special assembly for Independence day?

Divya : Lol. I was absent that day. Tell me something about her apperance.

Ahaan : She has long hair, is short in height, does not wear glasses I guess and... that's it.

Divya : Wait. Let me find out who conducted the assembly.

I waited.

Divya : There were two girls, Shreya Agarwal and Aanya jain.

Ahaan : Oh! Then she must be Aanya.

Divya : Wait. I have her photograph.

Divya : (Sent a photo)

Ahaan : Yeah. She is the one.

I instantly saved that photo.

Divya : By the way, what happened?

Ahaan : Actually... I like this girl. I had a crush on her since August.

Divya : Oh! Nice. Good to see that you're in love again (She knew about my past).

I quickly searched for her ID and sent her a friend request. I messaged Divya again.

Ahaan : Thank you.

Divya : Aye! Just relax. No problem.

Ahaan : No. Really, thank you.

Divya : Relax and Chill. By the way, I must appreciate.

Ahaan : For what?

Divya : You have a great choice.

Ahaan : In terms of?

Divya : I meant to say that Aanya is a very good choice for you. As far as I know her, she's nice but a little introvert.

Ahaan : I like introvert girls only.

Divya : By the way, she's in 11th.

Ahaan : I thought she was in 12th. Humanities section.

Divya : No. She's a commerce student.

Ahaan : Oh!

Divya : Should I talk to her about you?

Ahaan : But how?

Divya : Easy. I'll just go and talk to her and in between, I'll drop some hints about you.

Ahaan : And then I'll come? And you'll praise me in front of her? Right?

Divya : Right.

Ahaan : Can be a idea.

After discussing this idea, we made a plan that Divya will go to her and talk to her at lunch time. After 5 minutes, I'll enter the conversation and she'll introduce me to her.

4
Portrait

A week passed. Me and Divya made a plan but we were not able to execute it because I was tensed and very nervous. All the boys will agree that we all are afraid to talk to girls. By the way, the friend request I sent her was not accepted till now.

It was Sunday and I was studying. Suddenly my mother came to my room. She was looking very happy.

"Look. The school has posted the photographs of quiz competition won by Jhanvi, on their Facebook page.", she said.

Jhanvi, my sister, recently won a quiz competition at school and our school's Facebook page had uploaded her photo in order to congratulate her.

"Nice.", I replied.

Of course, to avoid my studies, I started scrolling through Facebook. I scrolled and found a photograph of a girl. Yes, she was Aanya. At that time, I didn't react much because my mother was standing beside me. As soon as she left, I opened Facebook and searched for her photograph. I found it and instantly took a screenshot.

Keeping a photograph of your loved ones in your phone, wallet or phone cover and looking at them when you miss them is the very first sign that you're in love with them. I could see that sign inside me. I used to look at her photo after every 30-40 minutes.

♡♡♡

The very next day, at 5 PM, I was getting bored. So I decided to do something and I came up with an idea to draw. But the question was 'What should I draw?'. So, I decided to make a portrait and I think we all know, whose portrait I was going to make. I took out my drawing file and other material and started drawing.

It took me 2 hours to complete that portrait. I took a photograph of that portrait and sent it immediately to Divya to see her reaction.

After 10-15 minutes.

Divya : It's beautiful. 5 out of 5.

Ahaan : Thank you. I hope she likes it too.

Divya : Wait. Let me send this to her.

Ahaan : No.

Divya : Why?

Ahaan : I didn't have her consent for this portrait. It'll be awkward for her.

Divya : Relax. I'll tell her that I have a friend who makes portraits. He asked me for a photograph. So, I gave him yours. Simple.

Ahaan : Just make sure there is no problem.

Divya : Relax relax. Don't worry.

Divya : Done. I'll send you her reaction when she'll reply.

Ahaan : Okay.

And that screenshot took a lot of time. I literally waited for 2 hours. Infact, I didn't ate anything.

Divya : (Sent a photo)

It was the screenshot.

Divya : (Sent a photo)

Aanya : Wow *Didi*. It's awesome.

That screenshot made my whole day. It literally made me happy and my happiness was justified though. Just imagine, you do something for your favourite person and that person, who doesn't even know you, praises you. What an amazing day.

5
Eye contact

The portrait was done but now I was wondering how to make it reach Aanya. I again messaged Divya. I thought she must be annoyed by me now.

Ahaan : Hi.

She replied within a few minutes.

Divya : Hey.

Ahaan : Actually I want this portrait to reach Aanya.

Divya : Should I give it to her?

Ahaan : But then how will I meet her?

Divya : So come along with me. I'll also introduce you to her.

Ahaan : Okay. So tomorrow? Lunch break?

Divya : Done.

I must have said yes to meet her but I was still very nervous. The whole night I just thought about what I would say and do, when I meet her. The next day, I woke up and started gettting ready for school. Usually I take nearly 20 minutes to get ready but that day it took me a complete hour to get ready. I went to school and I was waiting for the lunch break to start.

♡♡♡

Bell rings. I rushed towards the ground. I also took one of my friends, Akshat Kumar with me. We both started searching for Divya but we couldn't find her anywhere.

After a few minutes, Akshat came running towards me and said, "I just talked to her classmate. She's absent."

It was Saturday and I couldn't wait for two more days to see Aanya. So, I decided to give that portrait to her myself. I found her after searching for about 5 minutes but I was scared. I was very tense and nervous.

Bell rings again. Lunch break was over but I still didn't have enough confidence to face her.

"You're a coward.", said Akshat.

"What?", I asked.

"You don't have enough courage to go and talk to a girl. You're gay, Ahaan."

"Seriously? Now wait. Just follow me."

My male ego was way too big. So, I turned on my alpha male character and went straight towards her. She was there with her 4-5 friends.

"Excuse me. Aanya.", I said but she didn't listen. So I repeated, "Excuse me. Aanya."

This time she listened. She looked at me with her dark brown, adorable and innocent eyes and my alpha male character instantly vanished there. That eye contact was just like in the fictional books.

"Yes?", she asked. Her voice was very peaceful and sweet.

"I am Divya's friend.", I said but she looked confused.

"Portrait maker.", I explained.

"Oh!"

I took out that portrait from my pocket and gave it to her.

"Thank you.", she replied.

"Relax. It's okay. No problem.", nervousness was clearly visible on my face. She turned and started leaving but I didn't want her to leave. So I called her again.

"Aanya."

She turned back towards me.

"Yes?"

"Do you read poetry?"

Yes, I write poems.

She said no by shaking her head.

"Okay. Actually I write poems. Will you read them?", I said.

"Okay.", she said with a slight smile on her face.

She again turned back and left.

OMG! Those eyes.

The whole time, I was talking to her, I was looking at her eyes and her eyes were as beautiful as her whole face. I was able to see myself in those eyes. The best eyes I have ever seen so far. If there was a quote dedicated to her eyes then it would be, 'I don't know, what the value of eyes is, but your eyes are valuable enough that I would even sacrifice my life for them.'

6
A Secret

After giving her the portrait, I went to my classroom. It was English period. I entered and saw Dhiraj, Farhan and Karan looking at me very strangely. I went there and asked, "What happened?"

"Now will you keep a secret from us too?", asked Karan.

"Ofcourse he will. He is a big man now.", said Dhiraj.

"Which secret?", I asked.

"Who's Aanya?", asked Karan.

Our English teacher, Mrs. Priya Pandey entered the classroom. We wished her good morning and sat back on our seats. I was afraid that if I told my friends about Aanya, they would tell her that I love her. I think, we all know how male friendships are.

"Now tell us, who's Aanya?", asked Karan softly.

I replied, "Who told you about her?"

"Just tell us, you bastard."

"She's my family friend."

"He's lying.", said Dhiraj.

"No. I'm not."

"*Andi mandi shandi...*", said Farhan. Son of a bitch.

"Okay. I have a crush on her.", I spoke the truth. I explained the whole story to them. I told them all about that assembly, about Divya, about the portrait. After listening to my story, they started teasing me.

"So, when are you introducing us to *Bhabhi ji?*", Dhiraj asked. Again, just one of 'The Boys' things.

"Soon.", I replied because I thought things would start happening now.

Anant sir entered the class and spoke loudly, "Our school organizing picnic on 20th November. It is at *'Rajeev Palace'*. There is a Rs.1,000 of charge, which includes breakfast, travelling, lunch, other activities. Last date submission is 15th November. Give money to class teacher. That's it."

Such a terrible use of grammar.

I reached home at 3 o'clock in the afternoon and started waiting to see, when Aanya would accept my friend request and we'll talk. Not four, not five, but six hours had passed but she still had not accepted my request. But I thought it's okay. She might be busy with some work.

I received a message from Divya.

Divya : Hi.

Ahaan : Hey.

Divya : Are you going to the picnic?

Ahaan : I don't know. I have not decided yet.

Divya : Oh! By the way, Aanya is going. I thought, you should know this before deciding.

Ahaan : Okay. I am going now. Thanks for this information.

Divya : Nice.

Ahaan : But only if you promise me one thing.

Divya : What promise?

Ahaan : I want to get a photo clicked with her. Will you help me?

Divya : Why not? Just stay with me and I will get your photo clicked as soon as possible.

Ahaan : That's my girl.

After this conversation, I had already decided that I would definitely go to the picnic but I couldn't understand one thing. Aanya messaged Divya but she had not yet accepted my request. Was she ignoring me?

7
Picnic

On 19th November, me and my friends were planning for the picnic. At that time, we were sitting in a cafe. We just ordered *paneer tikka masala* and started waiting.

"So, what's the plan for tomorrow?", asked Dhiraj.

"What to plan? Just enjoy.", Karan replied.

"Let's do something crazy tomorrow.", Farhan said.

"What?", I questioned and then we all started thinking about something crazy to do on the picnic.

"What about bursting crackers there?", said Karan.

"Not a bad idea.", I replied.

"I have a better idea than that.", said Dhiraj mischievously. "Why don't we tell Aanya that Ahaan has a crush on her?"

Fuck.

"That's a good one.", Farhan appreciated that idea.

"No."

"Why not? We will tell her for sure.", said Karan.

"No please. We haven't even become proper friends yet."

"Okay. But only on one condition.", said Farhan.

"What condition?", I knew that he was going to demand for something stupid but still I asked.

"Accept that you are a son of more than one father or say out loud here that you're gay.", Farhan grinned and said and Karan and Dhiraj agreed to him and started laughing.

"Fuck you. I'm not scared of you all. Go and tell her."

"Okay. As you wish. Be ready for tomorrow.", Farhan laughed.

Our order arrived.

"By the way, the crackers plan is still active.", said Dhiraj while having a piece of *paneer* in his mouth.

"Okay. I'll bring the crackers.", said Karan.

"And I'll bring the matchsticks.", Farhan said.

"And what will Ahaan bring tomorrow?", Dhiraj asked.

"Some courage in his ass, I guess.", said Farhan and they all started laughing.

All male friends are bastards but the point is, there's no fun in living a life without them.

♥♥♥

The next day I woke up early in the morning, got ready, packed my bagpack and reached school. I was very happy because I was going to meet Aanya again that day. I was searching here and there for her and suddenly Anant sir shouted and said, "Children, be silence. Make line and start to move to the bus."

English language committed suicide.

We started moving towards the bus but I wished, I could see Aanya once but I couldn't. I entered the bus and my friends started rushing towards the back seat of the bus. They grabbed that seat and I also sat there. As soon as our bus started, I heard someone snoring. He was Farhan. I decided to woke him up but Dhiraj stopped me. He took out his water bottle and turned it over Farhan. He woke up.

"How are you feeling after having a bath after two months?", said Dhiraj.

"You are going on a picnic. Have some fun, Farhan.", Karan laughed and said.

"Well, it will be fun when Aanya finds out something about Ahaan today.", said Farhan and whole class started hooting. I thought, they would have forgotten but they told this to the whole class. Assholes.

ᗰᗰᗰ

We had a lot of fun on the way. We sang songs, danced and played a lot of games. We reached our picnic spot around 11 AM. We came out of the bus and took some photos. After some time, drums started playing to welcome us and we started dancing. We entered *'Rajeev Palace'* and it was really nice from inside. There were a lot of zones there. All the class teachers gathered the children of their respective classes and took them to the village zone.

"Find a place and put bag there.", Anant sir shouted.

My friends and I put our bags under a hut. Just then I saw that Aanya and her friends were keeping their bags in a hut which was just in front of ours. She was looking amazing but I panicked because what if, my friends see her?

"Dhiraj! Look there. That's Aanya.", said Karan.

After listening this, I knew I was fucked up.

"Let's go.", Farhan ordered.

"Hey, listen. Please don't go.", I pleased.

"Then call us *'papa'* first.", Farhan grinned and I didn't replied for the next twenty seconds.

"Let's go. I don't think he's going to say it.", Farhan said again.

Now there was a battle going on between my ego and my confidence and I let my ego win. I lost all of my confidence at that time. They all went to Aanya and said something to her but she didn't look surprised. She shook her head and my friends came back.

"What did she said?", I enquired.

"Nothing.", said Dhiraj.

"Call us *'papa'* first.", said Farhan.

"Just tell me, please. I'll give you a treat.", I replied.

Dhiraj was a foodie and I knew he would definitely do this for a treat. "Nothing. We just went and asked her whether she was Aanya or not and she shook her head. That's it."

I was able to see the disappointment of Karan's and Farhan's face. Hehe.

We went to many zones there, had breakfast, had a lot of fun but till now there was no trace of Divya. I started looking for her and found her after a couple of minutes. She was drinking water.

"Hi.", I greeted her.

"Hey."

"Aren't you forgetting something?"

"No, I guess.", she looked confused.

"Your promise."

"Oh! Yeah. But where's Aanya?"

"I don't know. Let's find her."

We started looking for her and found her after 5-10 minutes. She was taking pictures with her classmates. I looked at her and my heart started beating very fastly. I was able to feel the rush of blood inside me. I started feeling a little insecure about myself. I started questioning myself, 'Am I looking good enough?', 'Should I ask her about that friend request?', 'Do I smell good?' and many more.

"Hi.", Divya greeted Aanya.

"Hey.", she greeted her back.

"What are you doing?", Divya asked.

"Just capturing some pictures. Come let's click one together.", she took her phone out.

Divya looked towards me and said, "Come join us, Ahaan."

I went there. Aanya saw me and greeted me, "Hi."

"Hey."

She put on her sunglasses and we all clicked a photograph together. I wish she wasn't wearing those sunglasses, so I could see her endearing eyes once more. She started leaving but I called her, "Aanya."

"Yes?"

"You said that you'll read my poetry."

"Oh! Yeah. You also sent me a friend request, right?"

"Yeah. But you didn't accepted."

"Sorry. My bad. Actually I was..."

I interrupted, "It's okay. No problem."

"Okay. Then bye, I guess. My friends are waiting."

"Bye."

What a moment it was. I wasn't sure whether she would accept my request or not but after this meeting, I came to know that she wasn't ignoring me and I was very happy.

I was thinking all this when I heard the sound of crackers bursting and yeah, I knew whose job it was. I rushed towards the place from where sound came. I saw that Dhiraj, Karan and Farhan were being scolded by Anant sir and Ankita ma'am and to be honest, that scolding was justified but being a good friend, I went there and took their side. After getting scolded for nearly 20 minutes, we were spared.

ᗠᗠᗠ

After that, we had our lunch and enjoyed. We left *'Rajeev Palace'* at 3 PM and boarded our bus. I was tired, so I connected my earbuds to my phone, played some music and sat down on my seat with my eyes closed. The bus started and we started heading back towards our school.

After 10-15 minutes, I received a notification on my phone. I checked it.

Divya : (Sent a photo)

That was a photo of me, Aanya and Divya. I saved that photo.

Ahaan : Thanks a lot.

Divya : Aye! Just relax. No problem.

I started looking at that photo and just then, I got another notification. I read it.

'Aanya accepted your request.'

'Aanya started following you.'

I was speechless. I immediately accepted her request. I was very happy because a lot of good things happened that day and it beacme one of the memorable days of my life. I turned the music back on, closed my eyes and started thinking about Aanya.

8
First text

I reached my home at 6 PM. I went inside my room because I was very tired but then I thought of texting Aanya and my fatigue instantly disappeared. I messaged her. I haven't even changed my clothes yet.

Ahaan : Hey.

Ahaan : (Sent a PDF)

Ahaan : I have written these poems. Hope you like it and don't forget to leave your review.

After messaging her, I changed my clothes and had a sip of water. I took out my laptop and started filling my JEE form. After filling the form, I played my physics lecture on YouTube. I was not studying because I liked it, I was studying because our exams were going to start from next month. I completed the lecture in two hours and it's been about three hours, since I messaged Aanya.

My mother entered my room and asked, "Shall I serve you dinner?"

"Yes, please. I am feeling very hungry."

After ten minutes, my mom served me dinner. I was having dinner when I got a notification and it was, 'Aanya liked your message.'

Now I didn't even want to eat my dinner. To be very honest, I found it very rude and I started wondering why she did that. She should have replied politely. Or maybe she doesn't want to talk to me? I thought about messaging her but I didn't because what if she starts thinking that I am weird or clingy? Every child in their adolescence is a victim of overthinking and I was also one of them.

That night, my ego was telling me to never talk to her. On the other hand, my love was trying to covince me that she might be busy or tired and that's why she did that and while thinking about all of this, my brain fell asleep and I entered the world of dreams.

🖤🖤🖤

Two days later. Me and my friends were at the school canteen.

"What will you have, Ahaan?", Dhiraj asked.

"A kiss from Aanya, maybe." , said Farhan.

Speak of the devil. I saw Aanya and her four friends friends entering the canteen. By the way, I didn't message her after that day because I thought I would look desperate.

Aanya went directly towards the girl's section of the canteen. Even in school dress, she looked very beautiful. She ordered 5 sandwiches, took them and left. By luck, my friends didn't notice her there.

We ate *samosas* and left the canteen. As soon as we left, bell rang. We started heading towards our classroom. On our way back, I saw Anant sir scolding some girls. Aanya was one of them. It broke my heart. Seeing your crush being scolded or insulted hurts you a lot.

This time my luck didn't work. My friends saw her being scolded and they started teasing me.

"Go, Ahaan. Save her and be her hero.", Karan teased me.

"Smash Anant's face.", said Dhiraj.

"Give him a choke slam instead.", Farhan said.

Rascals.

💗💗💗

I reached home, freshened up and changed my clothes. I was having my lunch when I decided to text Aanya once again.

Ahaan : Hey.

I waited, and waited, and waited. I literally waited for four hours but the point is, when you're in love, waiting for them seems justified because when your wait ends, then you become the happiest person in your own world. The world of your dreams.

Aanya : Hiii.

I replied instantly. Self-respect left the chat.

Ahaan : Did you read my poems?

She disappeared. This time I was frustated. She replied me after four fucking hours, I replied within seconds and yet she disappeared.

She replied after 25-30 minutes.

Aanya : No. I haven't.

I decided to ignore her because why not? She also did the same with me. But I love her and once again my love for her controlled my ego and I replied to her texts.

Ahaan : Okay. By the way, today I saw you at the canteen.

Aanya : Oh!

Ahaan : And you were also being scolded by Anant sir today.

Aanya : Yeah! He's just so stupid.

Ahaan : I totally agree.

Aanya : Don't you think this school is boring as hell?

Ahaan : Well, it's my 14th year in this school.

Aanya : How are you still alive? Or maybe you're not and I am talking to your ghost.

Ahaan : I think time and place doesn't matter if you have the right company.

Aanya : Well, my friends are also boring.

I was writing something but she interrupted.

Aanya : Okay. I have to go now. Bye.

and she disappeared once again.

Ahaan : Bye.

She didn't even seen my message. I started questioning myself again.

'Am I boring?"

'Did I said something offensive?'

'Does she hate me?'

Ahh! This overthinking.

9
How to Cook?

It's been two weeks, since I talked to her and I hadn't messaged her since that day. She was nowhere to be seen even in the school. It made me a bit tensed.

I reached home and decided to message her.

Ahaan : Hey.

She used to reply late and I was used to it and I didn't wait. I started completing my physics homework.

After 10-15 minutes, she replied. Wow! Faster then I expected.

Aanya : Hiii.

Ahaan : Is everything okay? Because I have noticed that you're not coming to school from last two weeks.

Aanya : Yes, everything is fine. Don't worry.

At this moment, I felt a little awkward and started explaining myself to her.

Ahaan : Oh! Sorry. Actually I overthink a lot. It's a habit. Don't mind please.

Aanya : Gen-Z?

At that time, I thought she didn't like Gen-Z people.

Ahaan : No, no. I am not Gen-Z. I just have this bad habit to overthink a lot.

Aanya : Aye! Relax. It's okay.

Ahaan : You sound like Divya.

Aanya : Haha.

Ahaan : By the way, why aren't you coming to school?

Aanya : Because I am in Rajasthan.

Ahaan : You must be thirsty then. Have a sip of wat... Oh! Sorry. There's no water in Rajasthan.

Aanya : Haha. Very funny but I didn't laugh.

Ahaan : Okay.

Aanya : Relax. It was a good one. Don't start to overthink now.

Ahaan : It's like, kill someone and say sorry.

Aanya : Shut up!

Ahaan : Okay, *litti chokha* lover.

Aanya : What?

Ahaan : I heard that Rajasthani people like *litti chokha* very much.

Aanya : Are you dumb?

Ahaan : But why?

Aanya : It's *dal baati churma.*

Ahaan : But wasn't it from Bihar?

Aanya : You proved that you're dumb.

Ahaan : Okay. So, *dal baati churma* is the famous dish of Rajasthan and *litti chokha* is the famous dish of Bihar. Am I right now?

Aanya : Right. Now stop saying *dal baati churma.* It's my favourite and I am feeling hungry too.

Ahaan : I wish, at the moment you were here, at my home.

Aanya : What?

Ahaan : No, no. I mean I should have cooked it for you.

Aanya : You know how to cook?

Ahaan : Yes. I know.

I don't know how to cook. I lied to show off because girls like men who can cook. I only know, how to cook maggie and boil eggs.

Aanya : This was better than the previous joke.

Ahaan : It's true.

Aanya : Okay, I have to leave now. Ttyl (Talk to you later). Bye.

Ahaan : Okay, bye.

Although she didn't tell me to cook for her but when you're in love, you do everything to make your crush or partner happy. They become your center of gravity. You try to impress them in each and every way. So, I decided to make *dal baati churma* to show her that I know how to cook.

ღღღ

Next day, I started cooking. Now just imagine, a person who hadn't even cooked rice yet is going to make a complex dish like *dal baati churma.* It was very hard.

First of all, I searched for the recipe on Google. I found a video and learned how to cook. I noted all the ingredients on a piece of paper. I went inside the kitchen and started looking for those ingredients. I was only able to find only three of them in about half an hour. I didn't even know the difference between *Tuvaar dal, chana dal and moong dal.*

I called my mom for help.

"Are you sick? Why are you cooking? I'll make it for you.", she resisted.

"No, mom. I'll cook this."

"Who's the lucky girl?", she taunted me.

"Come on, mom. I am doing this so that I can improve myself. Now, can you please help me?"

"Okay."

She helped me in finding ingredients. She even taught me how to knead. That day I came to know about the real hardwork done by a mother to make her family peaceful and happy. Salute to all the mothers out there.

After two hours of cooking, we were ready to serve. I decorated the *thali* with *dal, baati and churma.* I took a picture of that and then I finally tasted it. *Dal* and *churma* were absolutely delicious. I didn't like *baati* much because I made them but it looked good from outside.

After eating it, I messaged Aanya.

Ahaan : (Sent a photo)

Ahaan : Well, I am a fan of this dish now.

And ofcourse, she took her time and replied me after thirty minutes.

Aanya : Wow! It's just perfect. Hat's off.

Ahaan : Thank you, thank you.

Practically, those six words were not enough to justify my hardwork but love isn't practical. It's magical. The hardwork I did made me praise myself because I was very happy and I said in my mind, 'Who's the best cook in this world? It's me.'

Gordon Ramsay be like, 'Should I leave my job then?'

10
Trust issues

"Four egg rolls, *bhaiya*.", Dhiraj ordered. Dhiraj, Karan and I were roaming on the scooty and then we decided to eat something. So Dhiraj, being a food lover, took us to this place called 'Raj rolls and momos'. Farhan was on his way.

"So, Ahaan. You got it or not?", Dhiraj placed his hand on my shoulder and asked.

"What?", I was confused.

"Aanya's ......", Dhiraj said and started laughing. Karan too started laughing.

"Hey! Be in your limits or I will smash your face.", ofcouse it made me angry.

"Oho! Being protective huh?", Karan teased me.

Dhiraj added, "Like a condom." and they both started laughing again.

I was feeling very angry but I acted cool and calm that time, showing them that I don't care.

Suddenly someone hit me behind my back. He was Farhan.

"Hello assholes. What's going on?"

"Nothing much. Someone is getting protective today.", Dhiraj said and after teasing me for another half an hour, they finally stopped.

I must say that if your friends know something personal about you, then you're fucked. They'll tease you, punish you, do stupid things with you but, when you will face a problem, they'll be the only ones who will stand with you and support you, and that's the real defination of male friendships, I guess.

Bell rings. Lunch break started. It was Tuesday. Me and my friends rushed towards the ground. We went to the canteen and Dhiraj ordered four cold drinks. We were drinking our drinks and talking about the test we were going to attempt in the fifth period.

We all started walking to go outside the canteen. I was talking to Farhan and I was completely focused while talking to him. Just then, someone bumped into me. My drink spilled on the ground and I got wet.

"Who's this idi....", I stopped. I saw Aanya there. She was the one who bumped into me. I got nervous and my friends were also there, looking at both of us.

"Sorry Ahaan."

"It's.. It's okay.", I stuttered.

"I spilled your drink. Should I buy you one?", she asked.

"No, no. It's fine."

"Okay. By the way, can you help me?"

I was confused, "What help?"

"Actually there's a lot of students outside girl's section. On the other hand, there are only a few boys at the boy's section. So, can you buy me a sandwich? I hate to wait and you can also have a drink. We'll have it together if you want."

I was completely shocked.

"But what about your friends?"

"Oh! Don't worry. They all are absent today. By the way, what about your friends?"

"That's okay. Wait let me introduce them to you."

My friends were standing there and I introduced them one by one, to her, "Aanya, meet Dhiraj, Farhan and Karan."

"Nice to meet you.", Dhiraj said.

"Me too.", she replied.

"Should we leave, Aanya?", I asked.

"But, your friends?"

"No, no *bhabhi*... I mean Aanya. You guys enjoy.", said Farhan and they left. Thank god they behaved well in front of her.

We both ordered two sandwiches and two cold drinks. One of them for both of us and ofcourse I paid the entire bill. She resisted it and wanted to split the bill. I too resisted and I finally won.

We went to the ground and sat on a bench.

"By the way, thank you for helping me and sorry for spilling your drink Ahaan.", she said.

"It's okay. Relax.", I smiled and said.

I was feeling very anxious that time. Just imagine, you're sitting with your crush on a bench, under a tree, eating sandwiches and talking to each other. So romantic, right?

"Should I tell you something interesting?", I broke the silence.

"Yes, sure.", she said while having a bite of her sandwich in her mouth.

"That day, when I made *dal baati churma*, and you appreciated me, I was blushing."

"Come on. It was really looking amazing."

"Thank you once again. Coming back to our story. Just then, my mom entered and asked me why I was blushing and I was speechless."

"You should have said that you were talking to your little sister."

What? She's not my sister, infact, I don't want her to be my sister. I love her.

"You're not my sister.", I defended my love.

"But I consider you as my brother.", she said, looking a bit confused.

It broke me. I started overthinking and at that time, I had no words. But I love her and I don't want to be her brother.

"Okay. So, the point is I love you Aanya. I have a crush on you from last three months and I don't know about your feelings towards me but I love you very much. So, please. Kindly, don't consider me as your brother because it hurts too much.", I proposed her in a very gentle way. My ego along with my love and my brain told me to do this and I did.

She was shocked. She became anxious and said, "I was just kidding but what was that?"

"Truth. It was a truth to be said someday."

"Okay. I don't know how to react. I am going.", she started leaving.

I called her, "Aanya! What's your answer? Is it a no? Or a yes?"

"My brain is literally not working. Meet me here tomorrow and I'll tell you. Bye", she said and left.

That whole day, I overthinked. I told my friends and Divya about this and they all were shocked. I again started questioning myself.

'What will she say?'

'Will she say yes or no?'
'What if she says no?'

ᗧᗧᗧ

Next day, I went there and started waiting for Aanya in lunch break. I waited and after 5 minutes, I saw her coming towards me. I was very nervous. My body started heating up and I started shivering a bit.

She finally reached and greeted me with a hello. I did the same and we both sat on that bench.

"Ahaan, listen.", she said softly.

"Yes?"

"Sorry, but it just can't happen because of too many reasons."

It broke me but I wanted to know more.

"Which reasons?"

"First of all, I don't know much about you. Secondly, I belong to Jain community and to be very practical, if we start dating today, it'll be of no use in the future because of the difference between our communities. In Jain community, a Jain can only marry a Jain. Third one.... let it be."

"Tell me, what you want to know about me and I'll tell you but I can't do anything about that community thing.", I tried to convince her. "And what's the third one?"

"My trust issues. I had a boyfriend in 10th standard and he left me. He used to flirt with other girls and when I complaint, he left me after saying that I was being too immature. I literally begged in front of him to not leave me but he didn't stop and one day, you'll also leave me, just like he did.", she said and started sobbing.

"Okay, Aanya listen. I am not going anywhere, okay? I am here with you. Don't cry.", I consoled her.

"It's okay, don't worry.", said smiled while sobbing and said.

"Bestfriends?", I asked because we all know that we can't afford to lose our loved ones. We can bear the pain of words or actions rather than pain of losing someone, we love.

"I don't even know you properly."

"No problem. You will, after spending some time with me."

She brought forward her pinky finger and said, "Friends! Okay?"

I accepted and crossed my pinky finger with hers.

"Okay. I should leave now. My friends must be waiting for me."

"Okay. Bye"

"Bye.", she said and left.

One special thing about schhol love is that we never stop trying. We are in love with our crush or partner so much that we cannot accept their rejection. And sometimes, it's better to not give up and fight for your love rather than just letting it go without even trying.

That time I agreed to be her friend but I love her and I won't give up. No matter what. I'll try.

11
Favourite singer

Time passed and our friendship became deeper. After that incident, she and I became very comfortable with each other. Now she used to message me first and also used to reply quickly. We used to talk to each other for hours. She also used to get jealous when I speak about any other girl.

She used to call me 'My hero' and I used to call her 'My little kitten' because she used to send me some cute reels of cats and their kittens on Instagram.

I also told her about my past relationship and how my heart got broken and since then, I never loved someone but she was the one who made me fall in love again.

I told her everything. How I saw her for the first time, conducting the assembly and then how I found her on Instagram, everything.

I also told my friends about that incident and ofcourse they made fun of me by saying 'katt gaya' and all other stuff.

ᗷᗷᗷ

One day, we were talking to each other on phone call.

"Hello, my little kitten.", I said while lying on my bed.

"Hey, my hero. What's up?"

"Nothing much. I was just thinking about you."

"Oh! What were you thinking?"

"Something I can't tell."

"Tell me or I am disconnecting the call."

"Okay, wait. I was thinking something dirtier. Do you want to know more?", I said and grinned.

"Shut up!", she laughed and said.

"What were you doing?"

"Nothing much. I was just listening to some songs."

"Oh! Nice. Which one?"

"Let it be. I have a very bad taste in music."

"Tell me or I am disconnecting the call.", I copied her.

"Okay. Bye."

"Your're such a shameless person."

She laughed and replied, "Haha. Okay. I was listening *'Lag ja gale'* by one and only, my favourite singer, *Lata Mangeshkar ji.*"

"And you say, you have a bad taste in music. It's a beautiful song, just like you."

"Shut up! In the last week, you have already called me beautiful a hundred times.", she blushed and said and yes, if you don't simp on your crush then what kind of crush is that?

"Why be shy in telling the truth?", I said and we both laughed together.

"Should I sing this song for you?", I said this because I liked singing and people also appreciated my singing. So I thought, 'Let's impress her.'

"Do you sing also?"

"Yes. I do."

"Okay. Then go on."

I got up from my bed. At first, I was very nervous but I sang for her with all my heart and she was listening very attentively.

.

.

.

.

"It was really really awesome. Such a melodious voice you have.", she appreciated me.

"Thank you."

"Well, I shouldn't say this but you are exactly like my ex.", she said and I was able to feel her seriousness.

No. No. No. No. Noooooooo.

"How?", I asked.

"He also used to sing, write poems, draw portraits and cook also."

Fuck.

"Okay. But no matter what, I will never leave you like he did."

"Well, I am not a big fan of the word 'forever' but let's see.", she said and the tension became normal. "Nevermind, you sang really well.", she smiled.

"Thanks. Are you okay?", I asked because I was tensed.

"Yes, I am. Don't worry."

I was not satisfied. So, I overthinked and explained myself.

"Okay, listen Aanya. First of all, I am not like your ex. I'll never leave you and secondly, no singing from now onwards."

"But why?"

"Because I don't want to be like your ex."

"You're dumb. Really, really dumb. I was just about to say that you're now my favourite singer."

"No. You're lying."

"No. I am not lying. You really sang well. I recorded it also."

"What?"

"Yes."

I took that as a compliment. It made me happy but still I resisted, "Please delete that. I am not a very good singer. You're ears will bleed."

"No. I am not going to delete it."

"Okay. As you wish."

"Yes, and never ever compare yourself to my ex. You are way too better than him. I trust you."

Not only my cheeks, but my entire body was blushing after hearing this. There's a lot of satisfaction when you know that the person you love, trusts you a lot.

"Okay. Thank you."

"Aye! Relax. Okay, now I have to go. My mom is calling me."

"Okay, bye."

"Bye."

12
In the middle

Aanya : Merry Christmas, my hero.

It was Christmas that day. I was studying when I recieved this message from Aanya.

Ahaan : Same to you, my little kitten.

Aanya : What were you doing?

Ahaan : Nothing much. I was watching a movie.

I lied because I wanted to talk to her. Well, love also makes you a liar because sometimes, you have to tell a lie in order to save your friendship or relationship or when you have to talk to them also. I know it's not okay to lie to your partner and all that stuff but when we are in school, we are not mature enough to know this properly.

Aanya : Okay. Then, bye. Enjoy your movie.

Ahaan : No. Wait. Movie can be paused.

Aanya : Okay.

Ahaan : What were you doing?

Aanya : Texting you :)

Ahaan : Oh! Yeah. I am dumb.

Aanya : Finally you accepted the truth.

Ahaan : So, what's your wish of the day?

Aanya : First you tell me.

Ahaan : No. Ladies first.

Aanya : Okay. Bye.

Ahaan : Okay, wait. This is not fair :(

Aanya : Haha. Now tell me.

Ahaan : I just wish that, on this new year, a beautiful girl wishes me a Happy New Year exactly at midnight.

By the way, Aanya sleeps between 10 PM to 10.30 PM everyday.

Aanya : Okay. I think I understood your statement.

Ahaan : What's your wish?

Aanya : You must not tell your wishes to anyone otherwise it would not be true.

Ahaan : You're a devil.

Aanya : Haha. I am.

Ahaan : Bye.

Aanya : Aye! Wait.

Ahaan : No, bye.

Aanya : Okay. Bye.

At that time, I was feeling a little angry but I controlled it and started studying again but I felt a little strange when she said that she understood my statement. I thought, 'Was she going to wish me on new year exactly at midnight? I don't think so because she was strict towards her sleep schedule. Nevermind, let's see.'

ᗞᗞᗞ

It was New year's eve. I, Dhiraj, Karan and Farhan were sitting and talking in a park.

"So, what's your new year resolution guys?", Dhiraj asked.

"My bad habit of sleeping too much needs to be improved.", Farhan replied.

"Impossible.", we all said together.

"And what's your resolution Dhiraj?", I asked.

"To stop jerking off too much."

"Cut it off.", Farhan replied and we all laughed.

"And what about you Ahaan?", Karan questioned.

"I haven't decided yet."

"To have sex with Aanya daily.", Farhan teased me.

"Shut up! I won't hear a word about her.", I replied angrily.

"Oho! Now she has become more important than us.", Karan said in a sarcastic manner.

"That's not the point. The point is.."

Farhan interrupted, "Listen Ahaan. If you want to stay in this group, you will have to tolerate our jokes. We didn't mean anything. We all are having fun."

"But do not include Aanya."

"Okay. Then fuck off. Go to your stupid bitch.", Farhan said.

This time my anger was at its peak. I got up and grabbed Farhan's collar.

"Leave me.", Farhan said.

I looked directly in his eyes and said, "I am warning you. If I hear anything bad about Aanya from your mouth again, I'll smash you and.."

Dhiraj came and separated us, "Stop fighting over a girl guys."

"Then tell him to not say anything about her again or he'll pay."

"Just fuck off, you dumbfuck."

"You know what, I don't want to be the part of this group anymore if you all are going to say anything terrible about her again."

"Let it be Ahaan. We don't mean anything", Karan tried to control the situation.

I was in the middle of love and friendship, so I took a decision. I contolled my anger and said, "I don't care what you mean and what you don't but I won't hear anything wrong about her again." and I left that park.

When you're in love, specially in your teenage, you sometimes take bad decisions and your decision revolves entirely around your hormones. You prioritize love over friends, family and career and that's not a mature way to act. One needs love but love needs a lot. When you make a bad decision, you suffer and suffering demands pain.

13
Dreamland

I reached my home at 7 PM. I was very angry at that time but I controlled my anger and went to the kitchen to eat something. Well, eating is a great way to reduce your stress and anger.

I entered the kitchen and saw my mom cooking something.

"What are you cooking mom?", I said while having a sip of water.

"Your favourite, *rajma chawal.*"

Rajma chawal is not a dish, it's an emotion. My anger instantly disapperared after hearing this.

"It's not only my favourite but the favourite of the entire India."

"Wait. It'll be ready in 30 minutes."

"Okay."

I went inside my room and started studying for my JEE exam.

Well, being a JEE aspirant is not easy at all. For all those who don't know about JEE, it's the second toughest exam in the world. You have to work hard, go through different emotions, face the distractions and most importantly, you must have passion and courage to pass this exam. That's how an IITian is made. Sounds horrible and tough right? But imagine, once you get into IIT, how proud your parents would be for you. You'll earn a lot of respect from the society and everyone will praise you. Now, it sounds like a dream.

My journey was also quite stressful. I was very excited at the beginning of the 11ᵗʰ class. I used to study a lot but after some 5-6 months, I started feeling less motivated and then, my life took a turn. I met Mithali, the topper of our school and we became very good friends of each other. After talking to her, I came to know that she was also facing a lot of problems and then, I decided to study hard and help her in her studies. After some time, we started dating each other. We shared a very beautiful bond. I used to teach her and help her a lot in her studies but then, we broke up. It was a very heartbreaking moment for me. I started feeling lonely and depressed. Well, teenage heartbrakes are the worst ones. I stopped studying and it took me 3-4 months to get out of that phase. Ishika, a very good friend of mine, helped me a lot in moving on. She supported me a lot in my journey. After that phase, I decided that one day I'll definitely become an IITian but I didn't think of studying. I was not able to focus for more than 20 minutes and after a short period of time, I became quite distracted.

After studying for two hours, I ate my dinner. I was in my room, watching a movie. My father, Mr. Sunil Sehgal entered my room. For your information, he's the coolest dad in the world except for my studies. He just wants me to study hard and get a decent job in the future.

"What are you doing?", he said in his deep voice.

"Watching a movie dad."

"Your JEE exam is coming near, so you should study."

Here we go again.

"But I just studied for straight two hours."

"Only a few months are left. Study, then it's just fun. I want you to crack IIT."

He said same in 9th and 10th standard too.

"Please dad. Let me take some rest."

"Okay. As you wish. I just want you to get good grades."

And he left.

When you are in your teenage, you and your parents become quite distant because of the generation gap and sometimes, it hurts a lot. Your parents do not expect much from you but when you're still not able to fulfill their expectations, it hurts a lot. They don't want anything from you except love, respect and some time. They work hard, just to see you successful and happy.

♡♡♡

It was 12.20 AM. I could hear the sounds of New Year celebrations. I could also hear fireworks going off outside. I thought of seeing fireworks and went to the terrace.

I took out my phone to capture the moment and I saw a message from Aanya.

Aanya : Happy New Year, my cutie. I wish this year brings you a lot of love, happiness, success and some brain, and I am not as beautiful as you say.

I received this message at exactly midnight and I was overwhelmed after reading it. She sacrificed her sleep just to wish me Happy New Year.

Ahaan : Same to you, my queen and you are more beautiful than you think. Just have a look from my eyes.

I messaged her and got a reply within ten seconds.

Aanya : Shut up :)

Ahaan : I thought you must have fallen asleep.

Aanya : No no. I was awake just to see what you would reply because your text messages make me feel special.

I really didn't expect this. I defitinely thought that she would wish me but I didn't think that she would even wait for my reply.

Ahaan : You are special for me.

Aanya ; Okay, enough of your compliments. I am feeling sleepy now.

Ahaan : Okay, bye. Good night.

Aanya : Why are you saying bye? I am coming in your dream, just wait.

Ahaan : Being flirty, huh?

Aanya : Shut up! Good night.

Ahaan : Good night.

I was feeling very special at that time. I didn't expect this much efforts from her. She's just so perfect and amazing and after that conversation, I was sure that who was going to visit in my dreams that night.

14
Exams

Exam time is never easy. You have to study hard and that's the most difficult thing for our entire generation because of too many distractions in our life.

My pre-boards were going to start from 10th January and my JEE Mains exam was on 30th January. It was quite a stressful time for me because I had to study very hard in order to crack my JEE Mains exam, but Aanya supported me a lot. She always tried to motivate me. Her exams were also going to start very soon.

I was trying to manage my studies along with my love but it's not as easy as it sounds. Love needs time but your goals need time too.

ᗡᗡᗡ

It was 10th January. That day I had my first pre-board exam of Physics. I was not completely prepared but I was ready. I was confident that I could do it.

At 8:15 AM, we got our question paper and I started looking at the questions. I found it moderate and started writing the answers on my answer sheet after 15 minutes of reading time.

Three hours were passed and our time was over. I was confident and I was thinking that I will get good marks in that exam.

Similarly, I also gave my Maths, Chemistry, English and IP exam and I was satisfied with my performance but the most important one, my JEE Mains exam was still not over yet.

♡♡♡

29th January, 2024. I was studying when I received a message from Aanya.

Aanya : Best of luck for your exam, my champ.

Ahaan : Thank you.

Aanya : Aye! No need to say thank you. I am always there for you.

Ahaan : Exactly! Thanks for being there with me whenever I needed you.

Aanya : Shut up!

Ahaan : Okay, ma'am.

Aanya : So, are you excited for your birthday?

My birthday comes on 31st January and being a boy, I hate my own birthday. I live it like a normal day.

Ahaan : Did you remember?

Aanya : Yes, I do.

Ahaan : I thought, you must have forgotten it. Well, I don't get excited about my birthday anymore.

Aanya : You're stupid :) Get back to your studies then.

Ahaan : Okay ma'am.

Aanya : And don't forget to give me a treat.

Ahaan : I'll give you a box full of sweets. Tell me your favourite sweet.

Aanya : I like *kaju katli* very much.

Ahaan : Okay, done ma'am.

Aanya : Now bye and stop calling me ma'am. I am blushing and my parents are sitting in front of me.

Ahaan : Bye ma'am :)

Aanya : Aghhh!

Ahaan : Haha.

Just then I received another message from my school group. Ankita ma'am had sent a notice.

'Dear parents,

There's a PTM tomorrow and it's compulsory to attend it as results of your ward will be shown to you.

Regards,

Class teacher'

I was scared and my feeling was justified though but I made myself calm and started studying again.

ᐁᐁᐁ

Next day, I woke up at 6 AM. I freshened up and started packing some important things like my admit card, pen and *aadhar* card and yes, I got the morning shift. I reached my exam center till 7.20 AM with my dad and after standing in a very long line for one hour, I finally entered the exam center.

After some biometric scans and verification, I was alloted a computer system. There were still 20 minutes left for the exam to start. I closed my eyes and started remembering some important people of my life, like, my dad, my mom, my grandparents and Aanya. I was missing her very much at that moment. If she was there, she would have relaxed me once again before the exam.

After some time, I heard an announcement.

'Dear candidates, you can now fill your details in your computer and your exam will automatically start after 5 minutues. Best of luck to all.'

I was very nervous at that time. I filled my details and started waiting for my exam to start. After 5 minutes, my exam started and I started solving questions.

Questions were way too tough and I was not able to solve them. Maths section was very tough and lengthy. Physics and Chemistry were moderate but still I was taking a lot of time to solve it.

Two hours had passed and I had attempted as much as I could. I was not able to solve more questions. I started getting angry at myself and started thinking, 'I wish I had studied for one more hour', 'I wish I had studied a few more topics', 'I wish I had taken one less scooty ride with my friends' and I started regretting my decisions.

'What will I tell my parents?'

'Will I be able to make my parents proud?'

'Everyone including Aanya will consider me a loser. Am I a loser?'

I started overthinking and after one more hour, our exam ended. I was only able to solve 25 questions and even if by any chance, I got 25 out of 25 questions coreect, I'll still not be able to clear the cut off.

I came out of the exam center. My dad was waiting for me.

"How was your exam?", he asked.

"It was moderate dad.", I lied.

"Will you be able to clear it?"

"Yes yes."

"Good."

It felt a lot more bad when I lied to my dad. In your teenage, when you tell a small lie to your parents, it does not feel so bad, but when it is about their expectations from us, then it definitely hurts a lot.

15
Regret

Regret is a very common thing. Everyone regrets about the bad decisions they make. Sometimes, it can be the ache of missed opportunities and sometimes, it can be the echo of words left unsaid. Regret weighs a lot on our hearts.

After giving my JEE Mains exam, I was sure that I would not be able to pass it. I started regretting about the decisions I made in the past. I started cursing myself and thought, 'I am a loser, who's not capable enough to fulfill his parents expectations. People will taunt me and how ashamed will my dad and mom be of me? What about Aanya? She'll also think that I am a loser, who's not capable of doing something. Everyone will feel so ashamed of me. I should die.'

Yes. That's how a boy feels when he thinks that he is of no use. A boy has to face a lot of problems in his life, especially in teenage, like loneliness, overthinking, heartbrakes, having trust issues, and sometimes betrayal too, but still he handles everything with a smile on his face.

᠊᠊᠊ ♥♥♥ ᠊᠊᠊

I reached my home at 1 PM in the afternoon. I was feeling way too low at that time. When I entered I saw my mom standing there.

"How was your exam?", she asked.

"It was good mom.", I lied again.

"Will you be able to pass it?"

"Yes mom. Now, please leave me alone. I am tired and I need to sleep."

"I attended your PTM today. You scored only 67%. Are you satisfied with your result?"

I got another shock.

"No mom. I am sorry. I'll study hard and definitely get good grades in the next exam.", I said and I was not able to maintain eye contact with her.

"Just do something that will make us feel proud of you."

"Okay mom."

I was feeling depressed at that time. I kept my phone aside after turning on 'Airplane mode' because I didn't want to talk to anyone, and after crying alone for straight one hour, I slept.

We all have heard that 'Men don't cry' but they do cry. They just don't want you to know because according to them, people will think that they are loser and they cry, just to get sympathy. No one wants to know about the emotions behind those tears.

ᐳᐳᐳ

Two days had passed, one of which was my birthday, but I had neither talked to anyone, including Aanya, nor turned on my phone. I started considering myself a loser. I was regretting that I wish I had studied a little.

I was overthinking but then I changed my mind. I was missing Aanya very much and I thought, talking to her would definitely improve my condition. I knew that she'll motivate me, encourage me and make me relax.

I turned off 'Airplane mode', turned on my internet and I was not shocked after seeing so much messages because of my birthday, which was a day before.

First of all, I opened Farhan's messages because I wanted to see, what he wants to say.

Farhan : Happy birthday Ahaan, my son, and sorry for what I did.

I replied.

Ahaan : Thank you and please do not to say anything about her again. I hope you understand, and you're my son and I am your dad. Be in your limits.

Similarly, Divya, Dhiraj, Karan and many others wished me a Happy Birthday but then, I saw a lot of messages I received from Aanya. I opened it.

Aanya (16:04) : Hey! How was your exam?

Aanya (20:38) : Are you alive or did you commit suicide after the exam?

Aanya (00:00) : Happy birthday, my hero. Thanks for being with me in my bad times. I love you very very much. You're one of those fictional men, girls crave for but don't leave me for those girls, okay? To be honest, you're the most important person to me after my family. I just wish that in future, your college should be somewhere nearby, so that you don't go away from me because when you are not with me, I feel lonely. I still remember, how you were holding my portrait and we met for the first time. I still remember, how we met on that picnic. I still remember your poetry. It was just so awesome. I still remember, how you sang my favourite song for me. I still remember that *dal baati churma* you cooked for me. No matter what, I'll always remember you as my best memory of my school life. If I hadn't had a heartbrake earlier, we might have been dating today, but to be honest, whatever we are today, is just perfect. Just always stay with me and never stop believing in me. We will fight all problems together and just remember, it's not you vs me, it's you and me against the problem. By the way, sorry for being rude at first. I know I was being rude towards you at first. Leave it. Happy birthday once again. Have a great day. Love you <3.

After reading this message, I literally had tears in my eyes. How caring she was for me. I continued reading.

Aanya (00:03) : Well, I don't know how to sing but this is for you. Try not to laugh at my singing :)

Aanya (00:04) : (Sent a voice recording)

She sent me a voice recording of her singing, *'Lag ja gale'*. I listened it while having tears in my eyes and it was awesome and so overwhelming for me.

Aanya (7:35) : I don't know where you are :(Please talk to me, if you are reading my messages from notification bar.

Aanya (10:06) : Why are you ignoring me? Have I done anything wrong? Tell me please. I am getting tensed.

Aanya (13:24) : (Missed a voice call)

After reading her messages, I realized that I made a very big mistake. She was constantly trying to contact me and I was ignoring her. I started feeling scared again. I instantly regretted my decision of not talking to her.

I messaged her instantly.

Ahaan : Hi. Thank you for wishing me and I was not ignoring you. I was feeling a little depressed because of.. let it be. I am sorry.

And I didn't get a reply after that. I waited for 10 hours, but still there was no reply. Now, it started making me tensed.

16
Me, you and problems

Four days had passed and Aanya still hadn't replied to me. I was tensed. I was not able to focus on my studies too. I started listening to sad songs and their lyrics also started becoming relatable to me. Infact, once I even got a hallucination of her. I was becoming way too mentally weak but then I thought of messaging Divya.

Ahaan : Hi. I need your help. It's urgent.

She replied me after 15 minutes.

Divya : What happened? Is everything okay?

I told her everything about what happened.

Divya : Oh! You do one thing, our practical exams start from tomorrow. So, you meet her during the lunch break.

Ahaan : Okay. I will.

I must have agreed but still I was very tensed.

♭♭♭

Next day, I went to the school to attend my Physics practical exam but I was eagerly waiting for the lunch break to start.

After some time, bell rang and I immediately left my examination room and headed towards the ground. I reached there and started waiting for Aanya. After 2-3 minutes, I saw her coming.

I went directly to her and said in a soft voice, "Aanya, listen."

She looked at me and her expressions changed instantly.

"Just leave me alone. I don't want to talk to you.", she said angrily and started leaving.

"Please."

She ignored me, so I said again, this time in a louder voice, "Please, Aanya."

She still ignored me, so I went closer to her and said, "That day, you were saying that it's not you vs me, it's you and me vs the problem. Now, what happened? Please, Aanya. I want to talk to you."

"Okay. Fine. Tell me what you want to say."

"I am sorry."

"Oh, you are sorry, really?"

"Yes, I am."

"Do you know how tensed I was?"

"I understand..."

She interrupted, "No, you don't. It was me, who was suffering while you were ignoring me."

"I have a reason."

"Oh! Really? Reason or excuse?"

"Reason."

"Okay, tell me."

I told her everything about what happened and why was I not seeing her messages.

"That's what happened."

"And you didn't even think to tell me?"

"I am sorry. I acted way too emotionally that time."

"It's okay to act emotionally sometimes but you should also consider other people emotions too before taking any step."

"I am sorry."

"Promise me, you won't do it again.", she crossed her arms and said.

"Promise, my little kitten."

She smiled and said, "Don't worry. I am here. If you would not have met me today, I would have texted you and solved the problem anyway."

"You are so precious to me. I wouldn't have let you go."

"Okay, my hero. Apology accepted. I shall leave now. My friends are waiting for me."

"Okay ma'am." I said and she started leaving.

I called her once again, "Aanya!"

"Yes?", she turned back.

And I started singing *'Lag ja gale'* for her and she did that. She came running towards me, hugged me and started crying.

"Do not do that again please. It was way too bad for me.", she said while crying.

"Okay. I promise."

Well, 90% of the promises made in teenage are not fulfilled because when we are in our adolescence, we make promises, based on our emotions but one can only try to keep their promise, everything else depends on the cicumstances.

At that moment, I decided that I will never break that promise and I'll never leave her again but promise are made either to be kept or to get broken. I was not aware about my future, so I think I did the right thing.

Well, school love isn't about the right thing. It's all about the emotions and hormones. In this age, love isn't practical, it's magical and emotional. We don't know much about love in this age but the most beautiful thing about school love is that, it's the purest form of love that ever exists.

Epilogue

After that incident, Aanya and Ahaan decided that from now on, they would study hard and get good grades. She became his motivation to study hard. They reduced their talking hours and replaced them with their study time.

After that, Ahaan started working hard. He improved himself for Aanya. He studied hard and performed well in his board exam. Now it was the turn of JEE Mains. He studied more harder and performed well in that too.

Aanya used to encourage her too much. She kept him motivated and supported him mentally in his studies. They used to talk to each other for only one hour a day. Ahaan always asks her to stay a little longer with him but Aanya knew that it would distract him from his studies. She was very strict and disciplined in her approach.

Aanya too wanted to talk to Ahaan, but she controlled her urge so that, Ahaan could study properly. She waited for 3-4 months for him and when his result was annouced, she was the one who was more happier than Ahaan himself.

Ahaan scored 98 percentile in his second attempt of JEE Mains. He scored 95.4% in his board exams. Luckily, by the grace of god, and having moral support from Aanya and by doing hard work, he scored All India Rank 6034 in JEE Advance and finally completed his dream to become an IITian.

He was very happy and her parents along with Aanya were also so much proud of him. He gifted Aanya, a box full of *kaju katli* as he promised. They both shared it together and spent some quality time with each other but there was one problem. Ahaan got admission in IIT Kanpur, which means he had to go to hostel now to continue his studies.

$$\heartsuit\heartsuit\heartsuit$$

Ahaan was about to leave the city. He was at the railway station, trying to assemble his luggage in his seat. Dhiraj, Farhan and Karan were also there, helping him.

Announcer announced-

'Respected passengers, listen carefully. Train number 147, going to Kanpur from Faridabad is about to leave in five minutes...'

"So, bye, I guess.", said Karan.

"Yeah."

They all hugged Ahaan together.

"Don't forget your real stepdads when you reach there.", said Farhan.

"Atleast say something nice. I am..."

"Ahaan", someone interrupted. Ahaan recognised the voice. She was Aanya.

Ahaan turned back.

"Ahaan.", said Aanya. She was breathing heavily.

"Aanya, relax.", Ahaan said.

Aanya hugged Ahaan very tightly.

"Stay in contact please. You know your promise right?"

"Yes, I do.", Ahaan said and hugged her back.

They both were crying. It seemed as if both did not want to leave each other but the sound of train intetrrupted them.

"Wait, let me show you something.", Ahaan said and took out his wallet from his back pocket. He showed Aanya her photo which was there in his wallet. Aanya started crying happily after seeing it.

"Don't cry Aanya. Please."

Announcer announced once again, 'Train number 147 going to Kanpur from Faridabad is leaving. Passengers must board the train.'

"I should leave now."

"Yes."

Ahaan started boarding the train but Aanya called her once again.

"Ahaan!"

"Yes?"

"I have something for you."

"What?"

She took out her handkerchief and said, "This is all I can give you at the moment."

Ahaan smiled and took that handkerchief and said, "Thank you. It's enough for me."

"I'll miss you Ahaan."

"I am going to miss you too."

Ahaan finally boarded the train and train left, leaving some beautiful memories and tears behind.

Thank you for reading the book. I hope you liked
it.

Coming Soon

Well, the story is not over yet. Ahaan is going to his college, and on the other hand, Aanya has also passed her 11ᵗʰ class. They decided to stay in contact with each other but will it be that easy?

Wait for the second part of this book, 'College Crush' to know what happens next in the story.

Coming soon.

More Books By Hiten Bareja

1. Perfect For Me - Available on wattpad.
2. Who killed Vanya? - Available on wattpad.